# little miss Shy

## by Roger Hargreaves

Little Miss Shy just couldn't help it.

Being shy that is.

She was terribly, desperately shy.

She was so shy it hurt.

Which is what they call painfully shy.

If any time at all anyone at all said anything at all to her, she blushed like a beetroot.

She lived all alone in a little house quite a long way from where you live.

In fact, quite a long way from where anybody lives.

Thimble Cottage!

Little Miss Shy was so shy she just couldn't bring herself to leave her little cottage.

She never went shopping!

The thought of walking into a shop and asking for something was absolutely terrifying.

So, she grew her own food in the garden of Thimble Cottage, and lived a very quiet life.

Very, very, very, very quiet indeed.

BANG! BANG! BANG!

Little Miss Shy, who was having breakfast in the kitchen of Thimble Cottage, dived under the table in terror.

But it was only the postman knocking at the door.

"Anybody home?" he called.

Little Miss Shy, under the table, put her hands over her ears and shut her eyes.

"She must be out," thought the postman to himself, and pushed the letter he was carrying under the door, and walked away.

Little Miss Shy waited, and waited, and waited until the sound of his footsteps had died away.

And then she waited some more.

In fact she spent most of that day under her kitchen table!

It was dark by the time little Miss Shy dared to come out.

There it was on the doormat. The very first letter she'd had in the whole of her life.

She opened it, cautiously.

It was from Mr Funny.

'YOU ARE INVITED'

said the letter,

'TO A PARTY'

it went on,

'ON SATURDAY'

it said,

'AT 3 O'CLOCK'.

It added,

'IT'S GOING TO BE FUN! FUN! FUN!'

Little Miss Shy was horrified!

She looked at the letter again.

"I can't go!" she thought.

"I CAN'T!"

"There'll be PEOPLE there!"

PEOPLE!

In the whole wide world there was absolutely nothing that frightened little Miss Shy as much as the thought of PEOPLE.

She worried about it all night long.

But, the following morning, she made a decision.

"I'll have to go," she thought.

"It wouldn't be polite not to!"

But, five minutes later she changed her mind.

And , five minutes later she changed her mind back again.

But, five minutes later, guess what happened?

That's right!

She didn't sleep that night at all.

The following day was Friday, and that Friday little Miss Shy changed her mind one hundred and forty four times.

That's how many five minutes there are in a day!

She was going to the party!

She wasn't going to the party!

She was going to the party!

She wasn't!

She was!

She wasn't!

She was!

It was a long day!

And that Friday night was even worse than Thursday night had been. She didn't sleep a wink. Not even half a wink.

Saturday morning came.

And went.

Saturday lunchtime came.

And went.

Little Miss Shy just couldn't eat a thing.

One o'clock in the afternoon came, and went.

Two o'clock in the afternoon came, and went.

And then three o'clock, the party time, came.

And went!

But poor little Miss Shy didn't!

She couldn't!

She just sat there.

A tear rolled down her cheek.

"Oh I do so wish I wasn't so shy," she sobbed.

Four o'clock came.

There was a loud knock at the door.

Little Miss Shy hid behind her chair.

The door opened.

And in walked Mr Funny.

"I knew you wouldn't come," he laughed, looking at her behind the chair.

"So," he went on, "I've come to take you!"

Little Miss Shy blushed and blushed and blushed.

"Come on," cried Mr Funny, seizing her by the hand. "You'll enjoy it once you're there!"

And he marched the blushing little lady off to his party.

Everybody was there!

Little Miss Shy didn't feel very well.

But, everybody talked to her, and everybody was very nice, and gradually, the longer the party lasted, bit by bit, little by little, eventually, guess what happened?

She stopped blushing.

And actually started to enjoy herself.

"Told you so," laughed Mr Funny.

Little Miss Shy nodded, and giggled.

She was having the time of her life!

And only blushing a bit.

And do you know who she met at the party?

Mr Quiet!

"I used to be shy like you," he said.

Little Miss Shy looked at him.

"I don't believe you," she giggled, and then she thought.

"Would you like to come to Thimble Cottage for tea tomorrow?" she said.

Mr Quiet looked at her.

"Me?" he said, blushing like a beetroot.

"Tea?" he said, blushing like two beetroots.

"Tomorrow?" he said, blushing like a whole sackful of beetroots.

And then he fainted!

## 3 Sixteen Beautiful Fridge Magnets – any 2 for £2.00!
inc.P&P

They're very special collector's items!
Simply tick your first and second* choices from the list below
of any 2 characters!

### 1st Choice
- ☐ Mr. Happy
- ☐ Mr. Lazy
- ☐ Mr. Topsy-Turvy
- ☐ Mr. Bounce
- ☐ Mr. Bump
- ☐ Mr. Small
- ☐ Mr. Snow
- ☐ Mr. Wrong
- ☐ Mr. Daydream
- ☐ Mr. Tickle
- ☐ Mr. Greedy
- ☐ Mr. Funny
- ☐ Little Miss Giggles
- ☐ Little Miss Splendid
- ☐ Little Miss Naughty
- ☐ Little Miss Sunshine

### 2nd Choice
- ☐ Mr. Happy
- ☐ Mr. Lazy
- ☐ Mr. Topsy-Turvy
- ☐ Mr. Bounce
- ☐ Mr. Bump
- ☐ Mr. Small
- ☐ Mr. Snow
- ☐ Mr. Wrong
- ☐ Mr. Daydream
- ☐ Mr. Tickle
- ☐ Mr. Greedy
- ☐ Mr. Funny
- ☐ Little Miss Giggles
- ☐ Little Miss Splendid
- ☐ Little Miss Naughty
- ☐ Little Miss Sunshine

*Only in case your first choice is out of stock.

**— TO BE COMPLETED BY AN ADULT —**

**To apply for any of these great offers, ask an adult to complete the coupon below and send it with
the appropriate payment and tokens, if needed, to MR. MEN OFFERS, PO BOX 7, MANCHESTER M19 2HD**

☐ Please send _____ Mr. Men Library case(s) and/or _____ Little Miss Library case(s) at £5.99 each inc P&P

☐ Please send a poster and door hanger as selected overleaf. I enclose six tokens plus a 50p coin for P&P

☐ Please send me _____ pair(s) of Mr. Men/Little Miss fridge magnets, as selected above at £2.00 inc P&P

**Fan's Name** _____

**Address** _____

_____ **Postcode** _____

**Date of Birth** _____

**Name of Parent/Guardian** _____

**Total amount enclosed £** _____

☐ **I enclose a cheque/postal order payable to Egmont Books Limited**

☐ **Please charge my MasterCard/Visa/Amex/Switch or Delta account** (delete as appropriate)

| | | | | | | | | | | | | | | | | | | | |
|--|--|--|--|--|--|--|--|--|--|--|--|--|--|--|--|--|--|--|--|

Card Number

**Expiry date** ___/___     **Signature** _____

Please allow 28 days for delivery. We reserve the right to change the terms of this offer at any time
but we offer a 14 day money back guarantee. This does not affect your statutory rights.

**MR.MEN**  **LITTLE MISS**
Mr. Men and Little Miss™ & ©Mrs. Roger Hargreaves

CUT ALONG DOTTED LINE AND RETURN THIS WHOLE PAGE